The Great Turkey Race

To Shelly, Lucille, Linda, Jessica, and Wayne—
the best lunch buddies ever!
—S.M.

For Cam and Rosie—my inspiration
—J.P.

ISBN 0-439-85930-1

Text copyright © 2006 by Steve Metzger
Illustrations copyright © 2006 by Jim Paillot

12 11 10 9 8 7 6 5 4 3   7 8 9 10 11/0

Printed in the U.S.A.
First printing, November 2006

The Great Turkey Race

by Steve Metzger
Illustrated by Jim Paillot

SCHOLASTIC INC.
New York Toronto London Auckland Sydney
Mexico City New Delhi Hong Kong Buenos Aires

It was a chilly day in November.

During a game of hide-and-seek, Ollie the turkey heard Farmer Kate talking to Farmer Joe.

"Who's going to be the Thanksgiving turkey this year?" Farmer Kate asked.

"I don't know," Farmer Joe replied. "But this turkey has to be very special."

Ollie's eyes opened wide.

"I'd better decide soon," Farmer Joe continued. "Thanksgiving is almost here."

Cassie and Wing crashed into Ollie. "We found you!" they shouted.

"You won't believe what I just heard!" said Ollie. "Farmer Joe is going to pick one of us to be the Thanksgiving turkey. He said you have to be special."

"Then it should be me!" Wing said. "I'm the coolest turkey!"

"No, I should be picked!" Cassie said. "I have the most colorful feathers."

"I've got it!" Ollie said. "Let's have a field
day with different sporting events. The winner
of each event gets a medal."

"Then we can show Farmer Joe who to
pick—" Cassie added, "the one who wins the
most medals!"

They quickly decided on the events. There would be running, throwing, dancing, an obstacle course, and high jumping.

Later that afternoon, the goats and horses began hanging banners and flags from tree to tree. The ducks took care of the drinks while the chickens knitted souvenir sweaters.

The next morning, Rooster crowed, "Cock-a-doodle-doo! Let the games begin!"

Cassie ran toward the barn with Ollie and Wing close behind. When they got there, the other farm animals were already waiting for them.

"The first event is the Turkey Trot," Pete the chicken announced. Ollie, Cassie, and Wing lined up.

"Ready, set . . . GO!" Pete shouted.

Cassie was in the lead, but slowed down to blow kisses to her friends. Ollie and Wing raced past her. As they got closer to the finish line, Wing pulled Ollie's sweatband down over his eyes.

"I can't see!" Ollie said.

Wing had won the race. As Pete handed him the first medal, Wing shouted, "I am the greatest!"

"No fair," Ollie whispered to Cassie as the pigs played "Turkey in the Straw."

Cassie won the bucket-throwing event. Then Ollie won the dancing competition doing his wild Turkey Mambo.

With two events to go, Ollie, Cassie, and Wing had one medal each.

"I'm going to win those next two medals," Wing said. "Then I'll be the Thanksgiving turkey."

"We'll just see about that, Mr. Cheater!" Cassie said.

A trumpet blew! "The obstacle course race will begin in 15 minutes!" Pete called out.

Wing and Ollie hurried over to the duck pond, but Cassie decided to rest for a moment. Farmer Joe and Farmer Kate strolled by.

"The animals sure are busy today," Farmer Kate said, "especially those silly turkeys."

"Well," Farmer Joe said, "one of them will be mighty tasty at next week's Thanksgiving dinner."

"Mighty tasty?!" Cassie shouted as she jumped up.

"So that's what happens to the Thanksgiving turkey! I'd better warn Ollie, but not that cheater Wing. He makes me so mad." She raced over to the duck pond.

"Don't win any more medals,"
Cassie said to Ollie.
    "Why not?"
    "The Thanksgiving
turkey is going to be cooked!"

"Oh, no! That's terrible!"
Ollie said. "But what about the last
two field-day events?"

"If Wing wants to win so much,"
Cassie replied, "we'll just let him."

"Time for the obstacle course!" Pete said. "Follow the path from the pigpen to Farmer Joe's tractor. The winner is the first one to reach the top."

"Let's get started," Wing said. "I can't wait to win."

"Ready, set . . . GO!" Pete called out.

The three turkeys went through the pigpen,

over the haystacks,

across the clothesline,

and onto Farmer Joe's tractor.

"Hooray for me!" Wing shouted. "Only one more medal to go!"

Cassie and Ollie looked at each other. They felt bad about Wing.

"Please come down from the tractor, Wing," Cassie said. "We have something to tell you."

"Yes, yes," Wing replied. "You think I'm wonderful."

Cassie told Wing what really happens to the Thanksgiving turkey.

"What? Are you sure?" Wing yelled. "I don't want to be Thanksgiving dinner. Here, take my medals."

"Calm down, Wing," Ollie said. "Let's think for a minute."

After a few moments, Cassie shouted, "I've got it!" She whispered her idea to Ollie and Wing.

"Time for the high jump, our last event," Pete called out. "The turkey that jumps over the highest object wins."

Starting with a milk bucket,
Ollie, Cassie, and Wing quickly
moved on to jumping over a
rocking chair, a bale of hay,
and a cornstalk.

"I guess it's a three-way tie," Pete said. "There's nothing left to jump over."

"I see one more thing," Cassie said as she pointed to the fence surrounding the farm.

"Ready, set . . . GO!" Pete called out. Ollie, Wing, and Cassie raced for the fence. They jumped at exactly the same time and just barely made it over the top.

"Come back and get your medals!" Pete called out.
"But the three turkeys kept right on running…and running…and running.

And as for Thanksgiving dinner...
Farmer Joe and Farmer Kate ate the
most delicious vegetable stew.